About Family

I am always so proud each year to share the incredible progress being made by the Stefanie Spielman Fund for Breast Cancer Research at The Ohio State University Comprehensive Cancer Center – Arthur G. James Cancer Hospital and Richard J. Solove Research Institute (OSUCCC – James). The clinicians and researchers work tirelessly every day to develop new and innovative treatment options for patients through research, drug development, and clinical trials. This would not be possible without the incredible support of our Columbus community and from friends across the country that share my family's commitment.

Family is very important to me. My family is not family, but the team of doctors, nurses, caregivers, and staff at the OSUCCC – James and those of you that have joined me in the fight against cancer. We faced Stefanie's battle as a family. It wasn't her cancer, it was our cancer. We fought tirelessly trying to beat this dreaded foe and while we suffered a great loss when she passed, we continue to fight for a cure. We haven't yet defeated cancer and I don't want my daughters, nieces, mother, sisters-in-law, friends, or any others to hear the words, "you have breast cancer."

By purchasing this book, you are now part of our family so, thank you! Together, we will create a cancer-free world.

God Bless,
Chris Spielman

NOVEMBER 17, 1979 WILL ALWAYS BE THE DAY THE OHIO STATE - MICHIGAN GAME CAME ALIVE FOR ME. THOSE MAGICAL MEMORIES ARE AS FRESH TODAY AS THEY WERE IN MY CHILDHOOD. I DEDICATE THIS BOOK TO MY BROTHER, RAJ, WHO IS THE BEST BROTHER ANYONE COULD EVER WISH FOR. THANK YOU FOR FILLING MY LIFE WITH DREAMS. I ALSO DEDICATE THIS BOOK TO MY WIFE, ANYA, AND MY DAUGHTERS, EMERSON ELIZABETH AND MAEVE ANNE PARKER, WHO CONTINUALLY CREATE MOMENTS THAT I CHERISH EVERY DAY. I AM SO BLESSED TO SHARE MY LIFE AND MY TRADITIONS WITH THOSE I LOVE THE MOST. WITH THEIR SUPPORT, ANYTHING IS POSSIBLE.

Foreword by Ray Ellis

Finally there is a book to share with your kids and grandkids that captures the essence of the Ohio State - Michigan game and the passion that is Ohio State Football. Roy really provides you with the torch to pass down your passion for Ohio State and love for the Buckeyes from generation to generation. The emotion and pageantry of the 1979 Ohio State - Michigan game comes alive in this book.

1979 will always be a landmark year to my team, my family, and me. We faced many challenges that year as a team. The biggest change was having a new head coach, Earle Bruce. For Coach Bruce, following Coach Hayes was never going to be simple, as there was only one Woody Hayes. Our team not only had to adjust to new coaches and to a new system, but also to the fact that nearly everyone outside our program did not hold high expectations for the season. Fortunately, this was a special team that continued to believe in themselves and worked hard to accomplish their goals. I must point out that one of the heroes of this book is the late, great, Todd Bell (#25). He was the epitome of the energetic leader and team player that made each of us work together and make our greatest dream become a reality. Roy's personal tale about his family and the role the Buckeyes played is quite heartwarming and surely reaches across the many different families and diverse cultures alike that make up our terrific fan base. I hope you enjoy sharing *The Buckeye Block Party* with your family as much as I did.

Ray Ellis
Safety, 1979 Ohio State Buckeyes
1979 B1G 10 Champions

www.mascotbooks.com

The Buckeye Block Party

For more information, please contact:
Mascot Books
560 Herndon Parkway #120
Herndon, VA 20170
info@mascotbooks.com

CPSIA Code: PRT1014A
ISBN-13: 9781620864654

Trademarks are Officially licensed by The Ohio State University.

Printed in the United States

THE BUCKEYE BLOCK PARTY ™

Written By

Roy C. Roychoudhury

The Ohio State University
Class of 1994

Illustrations By

Lydia Ferron

What's the big deal? I thought. *This Ohio State – Michigan game and the whole week really stinks.* My family always acted like this was the most fun week of the whole year, but it wasn't fun to me!

Every year, everyone was certain that our Buckeyes would win the game and go to the Rose Bowl. Every year that I remember, I got so excited for the big game and all of the buildup for the special day.

Every year, I was sure we would win. Every year as I watched, something bad would happen to my Buckeyes. We would lose and **NOT go to the Rose Bowl.** I was done getting excited for this game!

Then came 1970 and the **BUCKEYE BLOCK PARTY**. From that day on, the Ohio State - Michigan week would always be **THE biggest deal to me.**

BEAT MICHIGAN AND GO TO ROSE BOWL

My whole family loved the Buckeyes. Even though my mama and dad came from different countries, once they moved to Ohio, they quickly learned about the Buckeyes. It became our family tradition.

As soon as September came around, I knew it was Buckeye season!

We never missed a game as a family. Back then, most games were not on television, but they were all on the radio.

We listened to games on the radio no matter what we were doing. When we were outside the house on an autumn Saturday, we would always listen to the Buckeyes on our transistor radio.

When there was a really big game, we watched the Buckeyes on the television.

If the Buckeyes won a big game, and Mama and Dad said we were really good, we could stay up late and watch **The Woody Hayes Show** and the replay of the Ohio State game on WOSU, the university's public TV channel.

1979 was a big year of change for the Buckeyes. For the first time in a long time, Woody was not on the sidelines. Coach Bruce was now going to lead the team. Woody still loved the Buckeyes, but he was going to spend more time with his wife, Anne.

I was worried until my brother, Raj, told me that Coach Bruce was the best choice and that he went to Ohio State and played for Woody a long, long time ago.

No matter what, though, I was still kind of worried. We had not beaten Michigan in four years. I had been watching Ohio State football games since 1976, and I still had **NEVER** seen us score a touchdown against Michigan. I hoped Raj was right and Coach Bruce knew what he was doing.

On our mantel in the living room, I saw all sorts of glasses and cups and fun stuff that had the Buckeyes and the Rose Bowl on them. I watched the Rose Bowl every year, but I never saw the Buckeyes play in the game. *It must be something that just happened a long time ago but didn't happen anymore*, I thought.

We were so excited for the season to start and for the
Buckeyes to start playing for Coach Bruce. Whenever I
was at the store and saw a magazine with the Buckeyes
on it, I begged my mama to get it for me. She would
always get the magazines for me. Mama loved for me
to read! I loved to read about the Buckeyes!

DOZEN EGGS $.85

GALLON OF MILK $ 1.62

CHICKEN BREAST $.65 /LB

BACON $1.40/LB

BREAD $.45

I don't know who was more excited when the Buckeyes roared out of the tunnel for their first game playing for Coach Bruce, me or the team. Not many people believed in the Buckeyes that year because of the new coach, but Raj and I sure did. The Buckeyes looked great and won their first game against Syracuse. Then they won a close game against Minnesota. A trip to California was next to play UCLA. No one thought we could win that game.

We were going to have to play harder than ever before to beat UCLA. When Paul Campbell caught the winning touchdown pass, Raj and I jumped up at the exact same time! We got so excited, we actually did this new thing we learned called the "high-five."

The team carried Coach Bruce off the field. That was the moment I knew that the players believed in Coach Bruce as much as I did. This season was going to be special. I knew it.

Every Saturday, the Buckeyes continued to win. Week after week, we enjoyed watching our Buckeyes play and win! After we listened to the Buckeyes beat Iowa on the radio, finally it was the week I had been looking forward to and dreading at the same time. It was **MICHIGAN WEEK**. Would it finally be different?

Not only could we beat Michigan, but if we won, we would go to the **Rose Bowl**. I remember Woody once saying that anything worth doing is not going to be easy. He was right. This was not going to be easy. All I could think about all week was the **MICHIGAN GAME** and the **Rose Bowl**.

The night before the game, Raj and I talked about the game until we fell asleep, and then I dreamed about the game. Could we win? Could we even score a touchdown against Michigan? Could we really go to the Rose Bowl? I couldn't even imagine that! Saturday morning could not get here fast enough!

GAMEDAY finally arrived. I was up before anyone, even Raj. I could not wait for the game to begin. It was only five hours away, but it seemed like five years. It just felt different this year. This was going to be special. I was trying not to get too excited. Would I be disappointed again? When I saw Coach Bruce and the Buckeyes on the field before the game, I felt as if Raj and I were standing right there with the team leading up to kickoff. **GAMEDAY** was never this **FUN**.

When the game started, the Buckeyes played really hard in the first quarter, but we couldn't score a touchdown. When the Buckeyes stopped Michigan **COLD** on 4th and 1 to complete a goal line stand, Raj and I started jumping and jumping and **high·fiving**.

Then came the second quarter and again, the Buckeyes played really hard but we couldn't score a touchdown. We kicked a field goal to take a 3-0 lead, but then Michigan threw a long touchdown pass.

Oh no, I thought. *Not again. Not again this year! How can this happen again?*

Then came the third quarter. The Buckeyes got the ball on the Michigan 18-yard line. Could it finally happen? Our quarterback dropped back, and he threw the ball. Could this be the moment? Could this be the play?

A Michigan player was going to catch the ball! It went through his hands, went high in the air, and Chuck Hunter jumped up and caught the ball. **TOUCHDOWN BUCKEYES!** My brother and I were jumping and hugging and jumping and hugging. Finally, we did it! We scored a touchdown! But, we still needed to win the game.

In the fourth quarter, we were still losing to Michigan 15-12. Michigan had to punt the ball. The Buckeyes lined up knowing they needed to make a big play and the announcer said, "Looks like they are coming after it." When Michigan snapped the ball, the Buckeyes stormed through the line and **BLOCKED** the kick.

The ball went high in the air. Todd Bell caught it and went running and skipping and running and skipping all the way to the end zone. **TOUCHDOWN BUCKEYES!** Raj and I were jumping and hugging and jumping and hugging. I don't ever remember us jumping and hugging like that before. We started saying over and over again, "Rose Bowl, Rose Bowl, Rose Bowl!"

The clock ticked down and we won the game 18-15. The team carried Coach Bruce off the field. The Buckeyes beat Michigan and I could not believe it. The band started playing ♪**California, here we come... Right back where we started from.**♪ All of the Buckeye cheerleaders and fans we saw were now wearing roses.

MICHIGAN 0 :00 OHIO STATE
15   QTR 4   18
TIME OUTS LEFT
DOWN TO GO BALL ON

That night was unlike any other. Not only did we score a touchdown versus Michigan, we won the game and we were going to the Rose Bowl! I had such a special day with Raj and the rest of my family. I finally understood why this week was so special. *I now know why this day is so much fun.*

We had a special **"BEAT MICHIGAN"** dinner that night. My dad said he had been waiting four years to be able to make this after we beat Michigan. We sat down as a family and watched the players celebrate on TV and talk about how much this game meant to them. I was tired, but happier than I had ever been.

I was excited for the Rose Bowl, but I knew I would never forget this Ohio State - Michigan game. How could I wait a whole year to celebrate the **NEXT Ohio State - Michigan week** and the **NEXT** and the **NEXT** and the **NEXT**? Every year, I knew I could look forward to that week.

If anyone ever asks you what is so special about the Ohio State - Michigan game, make sure to tell them about 1979 and the famous Ohio State - Michigan game which forever became known as the **BUCKEYE BLOCK PARTY**.

The Columb

Sunday, November 18, 1979

Buckeye's Blocked Punt Bea

About the Author

Roy C. Roychoudhury is a 1994 graduate of the Honors Accounting Program at The Ohio State University. Roy grew up in Marysville, Ohio, loving the Buckeyes. Whether it was counting down the months, days, minutes, then seconds to the Michigan game, or sitting on the edge of his seat listening to the Buckeyes on the radio with his brother, Roy has always had a strong passion for sports, and particularly the Buckeyes. The idea for these books germinated when Roy's youngest daughter, Maeve Anne Parker, was born. Roy's new mission was to put his older daughter, Emerson, who was two at the time, to bed each night. Emerson started to ask Roy to tell her stories, and Roy shared the tales and legends that he knew best. Emerson was riveted with each one. Some of her favorites included the 1979 Ohio State - Michigan game (now *The Buckeye Block Party*), the 1985 Ohio State - Iowa game, the 1986 Masters, and Game 6 of the 1975 World Series. Roy's wife finally suggested that other fans would probably be interested in these stories as well, so they contacted a publisher and started this journey. These are his first children's books. Roy has always had an uncanny memory for remembering minute details and facts about a multitude of games and statistics. He flexed these muscles when he won his only game show appearance on *Sports Geniuses* which aired on Fox Sports in 1999. Roy lives in Ashburn, Virginia with his wife, Anya, daughters, Emerson and Maeve Anne Parker, and dalmatians, Jaysi Mae and Sally. Roy thrives on running. He starts nearly every day with a five-mile jog. Starting in 2005, his dogs were his daily running buddies. Four years later, his daughters joined in the fun. In the true spirit of Woody Hayes, neither snow, nor rain, nor heat, nor fog, will stop him from completing his daily ritual.

For more information, please visit me at
www.buckeyekidsbooks.com

Have a book idea?

Contact us at:
Mascot Books
560 Herndon Parkway
Suite 120
Herndon, VA

info@mascotbooks.com | www.mascotbooks.com